ANIMALS TO THE RESCUE
AND OTHER STORIES

'You can't chop the tree down, Dad. The garden's perfect as it is!' shouted Sam.

'And then we'll fill in the pond, concrete the entire garden and turn it into a football pitch,' his father went on.

'See!' croaked the frog. 'I told you so. What are we going to do?'

Has the animals' worst nightmare come true? For weeks they have been worrying about the new owners of Willow Cottage and what they might do to the garden. Fortunately Sam's dad is only joking; but can they all settle down happily together?

AVRIL ROWLANDS is the author of many books for children. For Lion Publishing these include the popular *Tales from the Ark* series and *The Animals' Christmas*. Among Avril's hobbies are swimming, walking, theatre and steam railways.

Barnes Primary School

**In memory of Peanuts, a very
special cat who lived next door**

Animals
to the
Rescue
and other stories

Avril Rowlands

Illustrated by
Priscilla Lamont

LION
Children's Books

Text copyright © 2002 Avril Rowlands
Illustrations copyright © 2002 Priscilla Lamont
This edition copyright © 2002 Lion Publishing

The moral rights of the author and illustrator
have been asserted

Published by
Lion Publishing plc
Mayfield House, 256 Banbury Road,
Oxford OX2 7DH, England
www.lion-publishing.co.uk
ISBN 0 7459 4764 6

First edition 2002
10 9 8 7 6 5 4 3 2 1 0

Acknowledgments
With grateful thanks to Jonathan Bishop
and Alan Gregg, for their enthusiasm
and wealth of ideas during a day spent
gardening.

A catalogue record for this book is available
from the British Library

Typeset in 11.75/16 Baskerville BT
Printed and bound in Great Britain by
Cox & Wyman Ltd, Reading

Contents

1   Strangers at Willow Cottage   7

2   A Game of Cat and Mouse   16

3   The Squirrel Entertains   25

4   Out of the Frying Pan...   34

5   The Mole's Special Friend   42

6   The Biggest and the Best   50

7   The Runaway Rabbit   59

8   The Spiders Go to War   68

9   Animals to the Rescue   77

10   The Neighbours Come to Call   85

1
Strangers at Willow Cottage

'Peace at last!' squeaked the mouse, as the removal van pulled away from Willow Cottage. 'Good riddance! I'm glad to see the back of the Rigbys!'

'Why?' asked the worm, poking his head out of the ground. 'The Rigbys were always very pleasant to me. They never trod on me or said nasty things like, "Oh, look at that horrid, wriggly thing!" That's more than can be said for a lot of humans. Humans don't realize worms have feelings.'

'Worms don't have feelings,' said the blackbird, who was watching him from a nearby tree. '*Food* can't have feelings.'

The worm hurriedly burrowed back into the soil.

'It was the cats,' explained the mouse. 'The Rigbys had so many.'

'What's wrong with a few cats?' asked the worm,

reappearing further along the flower bed.

'Well, for a start, they eat mice,' the mouse said. 'And there weren't just a *few* cats. I'm sure there were at least six. I'm glad they've gone.'

'I'm glad too,' croaked the frog who lived in the pond at the bottom of the garden. 'They were planning to fill in our pond, and then where would we have been?'

'Homeless?' suggested the blackbird, flying down to pounce on the worm.

'Pondless?' asked the worm, sliding away to safety. He turned to look at the blackbird. 'Missed!' he shouted.

'You call that a pond?' the squirrel asked scornfully. 'I call it more of a puddle.'

'Whatever it is, it's our home,' the frog insisted. 'And Mr Rigby was going to turn it into a rockery. "Well, Froggy," I said to my husband when I heard the news, "well, Froggy, we'll just have to move, and at our time of life that won't be easy. We're not likely to find a pond of our own. We'll be forced to share one with newts and toads and all kinds of things." '

'And now you won't have to move at all,' said the snail comfortably.

'It wouldn't have been right to fill in the pond,' the frog went on. 'I don't go round threatening to turn their cottage into a pond and make them homeless, do I? Live and let live, that's what I say.'

'Whoever buys the cottage might still fill in the pond,' said the blackbird.

'That's just what I said to Froggy,' agreed the frog. ' "There's no knowing what new people might decide to do," I said. "They might drain the pond, cut down the willow tree, dig up the flower beds and concrete the entire place!" '

'A new family might, of course, be very nice,' said the old spider, busily spinning a web from the wall to the oak tree. 'They might like the garden. They might even improve it.'

'That's what Froggy says,' said the frog. ' "Look on the bright side," he says. But I like to be prepared for the worst.'

'They might like the garden, but will they like us?' said the blackbird gloomily. 'It is a worry.'

A week later a starling flew excitedly across the garden. 'There's a van turning into the drive of the house and a blue car following behind!'

'Do you think they're the new owners?' asked the blackbird.

'Do you think they've any cats?' asked the mouse.

'Well, my dears,' said the frog, 'we'll soon find out...'

'Hey, it's really old!' Sam exclaimed as he and a large collie dog jumped out of the car, quickly followed by

Matt and Katie, his older brother and sister. They stood and stared at the cottage while their parents began unloading luggage from the boot of the car.

Matt turned. 'You didn't tell us it was this old!' he said accusingly.

His mother sighed. 'Yes, we did. We even showed you photos, but you weren't really interested.'

'You didn't tell us it was right in the middle of the country, either,' moaned Matt.

'Yes, we did. Anyhow, it's exciting,' said his father, dumping a jumble of coats, boots and bedding into Matt's arms. 'It's a challenge. Now stop complaining and give us a hand.'

Katie raced up the drive. 'I want first choice of bedroom!' she shouted.

Sam ran after her. 'No, I do!'

The rest of the family followed them indoors.

'Well!' said the blackbird.

'Well!' said the starling.

'*Three* children,' said the frog, shaking her head.

'And a dog,' added a mole, popping his head up into the rose bed. 'We mustn't forget the dog.' The mole liked to be precise.

'I don't think we'll be able to,' said the starling gloomily as the dog raced around the garden, barking loudly at every animal, bird, insect, tree and bush that he passed.

'How do you do?' he barked at the squirrel. 'My name's Morgan.'

'How do *you* do?' the squirrel replied politely.

The dog didn't answer her.

'How do you do?' he barked at the mouse. 'I'm pleased to meet you. Name's Morgan.' He circled the lawn twice, then stopped, head on one side, tail wagging furiously.

'Not a bad size, not bad at all,' he barked happily. 'I'm going to enjoy my new garden.'

'Excuse me,' said the blackbird, flying down from the oak tree and flapping his wings in Morgan's face. 'But I want to make one thing clear right at the start. It's not *your* garden at all. It's mine.'

Morgan jumped in surprise. He knocked against the bird bath, upsetting water over a fat slug who was making a slow journey towards the vegetable patch.

'That's *my* bird bath you've upset,' said the blackbird. 'In my garden,' he added.

'It's not *your* bird bath,' snapped the starling. 'It's for all the birds. Otherwise it would be a *blackbird* bath. Blackbirds are always so selfish,' she complained to a passing sparrow.

Morgan backed away, lost his footing and fell into the pond.

'Froggy!' called the frog. 'Froggy! There's a dog in our pond!' She blew out her cheeks. 'Get out! Get out, you nasty great brute! Dogs aren't allowed in our pond!'

'Sorry,' said Morgan, scrambling out and shaking himself.

'You ought to be more careful,' sniffed the frog.

Morgan backed away. 'I only wanted to look round my new garden,' he said.

'This garden belongs to the slugs,' said the slug, busily eating his way through a tasty lettuce.

'No it doesn't,' said the starling. 'It belongs to the birds.' She turned to the blackbird. '*All* the birds,' she added smugly.

Arguments about who owned what were going on inside as well as outside the house.

'Mum...' said Sam, 'Katie's got the room I want. It's not fair.'

'She's older than you,' said his mother.

'And cleverer,' smirked Katie.

'No you're not.'

'Yes I am. And *much* more attractive.'

'I wouldn't want to look like you,' said Sam in disgust.

'Quiet, you two!' said Mrs Prentice. 'I don't want to hear any more about it. It's a really nice bedroom, Sam, even if it's small. And it looks out over the garden. You'll like that.'

'Do children always argue?' asked a wizened spider, who was spinning a complicated web in the corner of the living room.

'I think so,' said a fly, keeping a safe distance.

Sam gave up the quarrel.

'I'm going to look at the garden,' he said and went onto the patio. His eyes widened and his mouth dropped open. 'Oh wow!' he breathed. 'Wow!'

Katie followed him. 'It's beautiful!' she said.

'It's rather wild,' said her mother. 'There's a lot to be done.'

'It's perfect,' Katie insisted. 'You mustn't change it.' She ran across the lawn to the oak tree.

'You hear that?' said the blackbird. 'It's going to be all right. She doesn't want to change anything.'

'And I haven't seen any sign of cats,' said the mouse, beginning to relax.

'I'm going to build a tree house,' Katie called.

'Me too,' said Sam, running over to join her.

'No you're not,' said Katie. 'It'll be *my* tree house in *my* tree, and you can only come if I invite you.'

'I rather thought it was *my* tree,' said the blackbird huffily. 'But then, I'm only a blackbird.'

Matt came to the doorway.

'Well? What do you think?' asked his mother anxiously.

Matt looked around slowly. 'Cool,' he said at last.

Mrs Prentice smiled in relief.

'It might even be big enough for a game of football,' Matt went on.

'We'll have to see,' his mother replied. 'I think the removal men might be ready for a break. How about trying to find the kettle and making some tea? And has anyone seen Peanuts?' she added in a distracted voice as the family disappeared indoors.

For a moment there was silence.

'That dog's going to be a problem,' said the squirrel at last.

'Better than the Rigby's cats,' said the mouse.

'That's a matter of opinion,' said the blackbird. 'And what about that girl? Building a tree house in *my* tree! They all talk as if the garden belonged to them.'

'But it does, doesn't it?' asked the mole. 'They've bought it, haven't they?'

'I think,' said the old spider thoughtfully, 'that the garden doesn't only belong to the newcomers.' She stopped to tuck a stray thread tidily into her web. 'I think it belongs to all of us...'

'Except the worm,' the blackbird interrupted.

'The new family only *think* they own the garden,' the spider finished.

'Should we tell them?' asked the snail.

'Why bother?' said the spider. 'They wouldn't understand.' With that she caught up another loose thread, tucked it neatly away and settled down to sleep.

2

A Game of Cat and Mouse

'I'm sure I've seen a cat prowling around,' said the mouse, soon after the new family had moved in.

'You're imagining things,' said the starling. 'I've not seen any cats and I notice everything.'

The mouse was not convinced. That night he had bad dreams about monster cats, and the following day he searched the garden thoroughly. The animals, insects and birds watched him with interest and some amusement.

'I'm not scared of cats,' boasted the blackbird. 'I can't think why you are.'

'They'd eat me, that's why,' said the mouse.

'The blackbird would eat me if he could catch me,' said the worm, poking his head out of the soil.

'True enough,' agreed the blackbird.

'But he can't!' said the worm, slithering away to safety.

'If you're scared of cats, just let me know,' said the ant.

'You?' said the blackbird scornfully. 'What could you do?'

'I'll think of something,' said the ant. 'An army of ants can do a lot, you know. Just wait and see.'

The blackbird laughed so much that he fell off his branch.

Satisfied that the garden was safe, the mouse curled into a sunny spot by the patio wall and closed his eyes. He was very tired.

'Miaowwww…' came a voice from behind him.

The mouse shrieked, jumped high into the air and ran straight through the doorway into the cottage.

'Miaowww…' said the voice again, this time very close.

Shaking with fright, the mouse scuttled across the floor. He heard footsteps, took a flying leap onto a sofa and dived behind a cushion. There he lay as still as possible, despite a wildly beating heart, a twitching nose and quivering whiskers.

Mrs Prentice came into the room. The mouse peered out from his hiding place, but hid again when Mrs Prentice sat down on the sofa. She lifted the cushion to put behind her head and the mouse jumped… straight into her lap!

Mrs Prentice screamed. And screamed.

'It's a mouse! A mouse!'

Her screams could be heard right down the garden.

'Now's your chance to go to the rescue, ants,' said the blackbird sarcastically. And he laughed so much that he fell off his branch again.

'Right!' said the ant, turning to the other ants. 'In a straight line now. Behind me. That's it.' He walked up and down the line of ants. 'Now remember, our mission is to rescue the mouse! Forward march!'

The long column of ants solemnly filed across the patio and through the open door of Willow Cottage.

Mrs Prentice's screams had brought Matt and Sam running into the room.

'What's up, Mum?'

'What's happened?'

'It's a mouse!'

'Where is it?'

'I don't know. Somewhere! But get rid of it!' screeched Mrs Prentice. 'I won't have mice in the house!'

'Okay.'

Sam soon scooped up the mouse, who was cowering behind the bookcase, and put him in a cardboard box.

'Cool,' said Matt, staring at the mouse.

'Nothing to be frightened of, Mum,' said Sam soothingly.

'What shall we do with him?' asked Matt.

'I don't care,' said Mrs Prentice. 'Just take him away. A long, long way away.'

'He's really cute,' said Sam. 'Just look at his tiny paws and those big, beady eyes. Couldn't I keep him?'

'NO!'

'All right, all right. I'll take him to the fields. He's probably a field mouse.'

Sam put the box in a bag and hung it on the handlebar of his bike. Then he cycled out of the drive, along the lane and past the woods, until he came to the fields of Willow Valley Farm.

'I'd really like to keep you,' he said sadly, 'but Mum'd go mad.'

He put the box on the ground and turned it on its side. 'Off you go.'

The mouse took one uncertain step into the field and was instantly surrounded by a forest of golden wheat. It rose high above his head, cutting off his view.

However would he get home?

Back at Willow Cottage, the long line of ants had crossed the hallway and entered the kitchen.

'Mouse? Where are you mouse?' called the ant.

'Here, boss, just look!' said another ant in wonder. 'Food!'

'We're here to rescue the mouse,' said the first ant.

'But he isn't here, is he? You've called and called. He's probably gone back to the garden. But *we're* here and all these crumbs are here…'

The first ant wavered.

'All right then,' he said at last, and the column broke as every ant rushed to the nearest crumb. 'But keep it orderly! Pass the crumbs down the line! Steady now!'

'Who are you?' said a voice. The mouse shrank back. He was being stared at by dozens of inquisitive pairs of eyes.

'I'm a mouse.'

'We can see that for ourselves, but what sort of a mouse? You're not one of us. You're not a field mouse.'

'I live in a garden...' the mouse began, feeling quite weak with relief.

'Oh so you're a *garden* mouse,' said the field mouse sarcastically. 'And what's a garden mouse doing in the middle of a field? Why aren't you safe in your garden?'

'Well, it was an accident...'

'Oh an *accident*, was it?' said the field mouse. 'In a minute you'll be asking for our help.'

The rest of the field mice sniggered.

'Well, yes,' said the mouse. 'You see...'

'Why should we help you?'

'Because...'

'Don't you know it's very dangerous to come here?' the field mouse interrupted. 'There's all kinds of nasty things hiding in a field of wheat.'

The field mice murmured threateningly and moved closer. The mouse shrank back.

'We live by our wits,' said the field mouse. 'How do you live, in your nice comfortable garden?'

'Oh, er, by eating nuts and seeds and things,' said the mouse, confused.

The field mice began to laugh in a horrid sort of way, then stopped abruptly.

'Enemy,' said the field mouse and in an instant they had all disappeared from sight.

'Miaoww...' came a purring voice, right behind the mouse's ear.

The mouse turned.

'All right,' he said, too tired to run. 'All right. I give up.'

The cat stared in surprise. 'It's a mouse, isn't it?' he asked. 'You'll have to forgive me, but my eyesight's not as good as it was.'

'Yes,' said the mouse, frozen with fright. 'I'm a mouse. Just eat me quickly will you, so that I don't know much about it.' He closed his eyes, but opened them again when the cat spoke.

'Why should I be doing that, now? I'm not very partial to mice as it happens. Or anything that's alive. I'm too old and fat for hunting. And I prefer tinned food, so I'll not be eating you, if that's all right.'

'Oh yes,' said the mouse. 'Thank you.'

'Are you a field mouse?' asked the cat.

'No. I live at Willow Cottage.'

'Why, so do I! Now there's a coincidence! What are you doing so far from home, if you don't mind my asking?' said the cat, with a friendly smile.

The mouse poured out his story. When he had finished the cat sighed. 'Sure and I'm to blame in all this,' he said. 'I was the one who frightened you. I'm the Prentices' cat. My name's Peanuts. I'm Irish, you know.'

'I didn't think they had a cat.'

'Well, I haven't been out much. Grown lazy in my old age. Morgan's the one with the energy. Energy

but no brains. That's dogs for you. But there, it's been a fine day and I was thinking, Peanuts, it's time you had a bit of fresh air. Do a bit of exploring. Look round the neighbourhood. Walk off some of that fat.' He looked down at the mouse. 'I didn't mean to frighten the life out of you, to be sure. I'd better put things right, hadn't I?'

He bent his head, gently picked up the mouse by the scruff of his neck and set off down the road.

When they reached the garden, Peanuts put the mouse down carefully.

'There,' he said. 'You're not hurt, are you?'

The mouse stretched himself. 'No. I've been very stupid, being scared of cats. I won't be in future.'

'Now that's not at all sensible,' said Peanuts. 'You're wise to be cautious. But you can talk to me. Not all of us are bad.'

'And not all mice are good,' said the mouse, thinking of the field mice.

The cat stiffened suddenly. 'Was that a dog I heard?'

'It's probably Morgan.'

'No it's not. I know his bark. I can't say I fancy dogs as a rule so I'll go before he sniffs me out.' And he disappeared into the bushes without a sound.

'Oh so you're back,' said the ant, sleepily lying on a crumb of bread. 'We did come to your rescue, Mouse, but couldn't find you.'

'We found a load of food instead,' said another ant.

'Our reward,' said the first ant, even more sleepily, 'for a good deed.'

'Thank you,' said the mouse humbly. 'What kind friends I've got.'

Sam, looking out of the window, saw the flash of the mouse's tail as it ran across the patio, and smiled.

3

The Squirrel Entertains

'Look at me!' shouted the squirrel as she ran upside down along a thin branch of the willow tree.

'Why should I?' asked the slug. 'You're not as interesting as this leaf I'm eating.'

'Wheeeee...!' called the squirrel. She let go of the branch and jumped to another. 'I'm flying!'

'No, you're not,' said the blackbird. 'You need wings to fly.'

'All right, all right, I know,' snapped the squirrel. 'But couldn't you just say, "Oh, that's really clever of you," for once? Or, "My goodness, however did you do that?" A bit of interest and encouragement from time to time would be nice.'

'I don't see why. You're only doing something all squirrels can do,' said the blackbird. He nodded his head towards Sam, who was lying on his back in the long grass, watching the squirrel's every move. 'And *he's* showing plenty of interest if that's what you want.'

Just then Morgan came running out of the house. 'Time for my walk,' he barked happily.

'Ssh,' said Sam. 'See that squirrel? That's really clever.'

'There you are,' said the blackbird sourly. 'All the encouragement you need.'

The squirrel ran to the clothes line that stretched between two wooden posts and climbed swiftly up one of them. 'If you think that's clever, just watch this!' she called, then ran nimbly to and fro along the plastic-coated line.

'Oh wow!' Sam cried.

'Thank you,' said the squirrel.

'Show off,' said the slug sourly as he returned to his leaf.

Morgan jumped onto Sam's stomach. 'I know the squirrel's very clever,' he barked, 'but I'd really like a walk.'

'Oh get off, Morgan,' Sam said, pushing him away. 'I'm coming.'

A couple of hours later Matt was reluctantly helping his mother hang washing out on the line.

'Why did we have to move to a crumbling old house in the country?' he complained.

'It's not crumbling,' said Katie, who was sitting on the patio steps handing out washing from the basket. 'It's a lovely house, and I expect there are ghosts.'

'There aren't any, are there, Mum?' Sam asked, back in his favourite spot by the willow tree.

'Of course not. You know we had to move because of your father's job,' said Mrs Prentice.

'Yeah, but why Willow Cottage?'

'We thought the country would be nice. Ever since I went on a ramble as a child and found a four-leaved clover, I've wanted to live in the country.' Mrs Prentice looked down at Katie and ruffled her hair. 'I was about your age.'

'What's so good about a four-leaved clover?' Katie asked.

'They're very rare and if you find one, some people think it means good luck.'

'And did you?'

'What?'

'Have good luck.'

Mrs Prentice laughed. 'Of course. Didn't I marry your father and have you three horrors?'

'So who's going to do the garden?' Matt asked. 'I'm not, if that's what you're thinking.'

'Oh Matt, don't be so negative all the time. Another peg, please. We'll all do it.'

'Come off it, Mum! You and Dad don't know anything about gardening!'

'We'll learn. I've bought a book and I've been watching all the programmes on TV. And I was good with the window box we had in the flat. I grew all sorts of things.'

'Weeds,' jeered Matt.

Sam suddenly sat up. 'I'll help. I'd like to.'

'Thank you, Sam,' said his mother gratefully. She stopped and looked around. 'It is a bit of a jungle, though.'

The garden was bursting with flowers in full bloom. The apple and plum trees were starting to bow under the weight of their fruit, and the grass, sprinkled with daisies, buttercups and dandelions, was thick and tall. The flower beds needed weeding, while the rambling roses were busy climbing beyond the garden walls and up into the trees, where they fell through the branches in a shower of scented white blossom.

Mr Prentice emerged from the garden shed. He was covered in cobwebs. 'The Rigbys can't have touched the garden for months. Never mind, we'll just have to take an axe and chop it all down.'

The birds fluttered up from the trees anxiously.

'Did you hear that?' twittered the chaffinch.

'What about my nest?' asked a worried song thrush.

'You can't chop it down, Dad. The garden's perfect as it is!' shouted Sam.

'And then we'll fill in the pond, concrete the entire garden and turn it into a football pitch!' his father went on.

'See!' croaked the frog. 'I told you so! Didn't I say they'd fill in the pond and concrete everything? Didn't I? Oh whatever are we going to do? I've come over all of a tremble!' She dived into the pond with a loud splash.

'Ha, ha,' said Matt in a sarcastic voice. 'It's not big enough for a football pitch.'

'You're not really going to do that?' asked Sam, looking anxiously at his father. 'Are you?'

Mr Prentice tweaked his son's nose. 'Of course not. My idea of a joke.'

'Well, my dears, if that's a joke, I must say I think he's got a very odd sense of humour,' said the frog, emerging from the pond and sitting on a lilypad. 'But then I never get the point of jokes. Froggy's got a sense of humour, though. He's always laughing at me.'

The birds flew back to their nests and the family went in for tea.

Meanwhile the squirrel scampered back to the washing line and climbed up one of the posts.

'Bet you can't run along it now,' said the slug slyly. 'Not with all that washing.'

'Bet you I can,' said the squirrel.

She took one step, then another. The slug stopped eating and the birds peered down from the trees. Even the mouse, who was busy building a new nest, stopped for a moment.

The squirrel danced lightly over the first few pegs, reached halfway... Then a breeze caught the washing, the line swayed, the squirrel lost her balance...

... and fell...

... straight into one of Matt's red-and-white-striped football socks!

'Help!' came a muffled voice. 'Help!'

Only the tip of her frantically waving tail could be seen.

A loud croaking came from the direction of the pond. It was the frog. 'You know, that's really funny!'

'That's right,' said a bitter voice from inside the sock. 'Go ahead and laugh.'

A hand suddenly reached up to the washing. Sam

was on tiptoe, straining to unpeg the sock from the line.

'Just hold on a sec,' he said.

He stretched a bit further, his fingers feeling for the peg. He gave a pull... and the sock fell to the ground with a thud.

'Hey, wait!' Sam called.

But the squirrel had gone. Still stuck in the sock and unable to see where she was going, the squirrel hurtled across the lawn and disappeared under a pile of grass cuttings.

'Sam!'

'Okay, Mum!'

'Sam, your tea's getting cold!'

'Just a minute!'

Sam dug deep into the grass cuttings, but there was no sign of either the squirrel or Matt's red and white sock.

'SAM!'

'Coming!' He looked around. 'I suppose you'll be all right,' he said, and went indoors.

As soon as he had gone, grass flew in all directions and the squirrel emerged, without the sock, to cheers from the animals, insects and birds.

'That,' said the blackbird, flapping his wings, 'was the best entertainment I've had in a long time.'

'Yes, it was good, wasn't it?' the frog agreed, wheezing heavily. 'I must tell Froggy about it.'

'The way you dropped into that sock,' said the starling admiringly. 'Almost as if you meant to.'

'Well...' the squirrel began.

'And running across the lawn with it still on your head,' said the slug. 'Fantastic! I thought I'd die laughing.'

'Oh,' said the squirrel modestly, 'it was nothing. Nothing at all really. But it's very kind of you all. Thank you.'

The mouse was eyeing the sock longingly. 'If you're quite finished with it, would you... could you... let me have it? It would make a delightfully cosy home for my family.'

'Of course,' said the squirrel. 'Have it with my compliments. One can't perform the same trick twice.'

She smiled with satisfaction and went to her nest to eat some seeds. After all, she thought, she had deserved it.

So everyone at Willow Cottage was satisfied. Except for Matt who wondered where one of his favourite socks had gone.

4
Out of the Frying Pan...

The frogs who lived in the pond at the bottom of the garden were very proud of their son.

'Such a handsome froglet,' his mother would say fondly to her husband. 'Just like you, Froggy, when you were young.'

Ever since he was born, his parents had given their son whatever he wanted. They let him laze in the sun and swim in the shadiest parts of the pond. They tired themselves out searching for juicy water plants for him to eat. They admired everything he did and everything he said and thought him the cleverest tadpole that had ever lived.

Their son grew up thinking that too.

'He'll go far, you mark my words, Froggy,' the frog said proudly to her husband.

Their son did go far, especially when he changed

from a tadpole into a young frog, when he grew powerful legs and found that he could jump. He jumped out of the pond and all over the garden. He especially liked jumping on the other animals, insects and birds to give them a fright.

'Get that frog of yours out this minute!' shouted an angry blackbird when the young frog had jumped straight into his nest.

'Dear, dear,' croaked the frog comfortably. 'He's only young and his legs need exercise.'

The worm was equally upset when the young frog jumped on top of him, squashing him into the soil. The spider grew quite cross when he leaped straight through the fine web she had just spun. He even jumped onto the table on the patio, causing Mrs Prentice to spill her drink all over her new skirt.

'Maybe we should just fill in the pond,' threatened Mr Prentice.

Complaints about the young frog came thick and fast from the animals, insects and birds in the garden.

'If any of my chicks behaved that way, they'd have had a clip round the wing,' said the blackbird.

'He ought to be given a stern talking to,' said the squirrel, whose acorns had been scattered all round the garden.

'He just doesn't look where he's going,' complained the ant. 'He nearly squashed a whole column of us the other day.'

'He *has* squashed me,' said the worm. 'It was a good job he didn't land on my head.'

'It wouldn't have made any difference to your brains,' said the blackbird. 'You haven't any.'

'That froglet thinks he's the bee's knees and the cat's whiskers,' said the mole, wrinkling up his nose.

'And what's that supposed to mean?' asked the blackbird.

'I don't know,' admitted the mole. 'It was just something I heard the humans say.'

'You shouldn't go round repeating what humans say,' said the blackbird.

'I'm not sure I have any knees, anyway,' said the bee.

'That froglet needs to be taught a lesson,' said the squirrel, chasing after her scattered acorns. 'He's quite spoilt.'

The frog, who overheard, puffed out her cheeks. 'My froglet is not spoilt,' she said stoutly.

'He is,' said the blackbird. 'Look at the upset he's caused everyone. And has he apologized? Has he said he was sorry? Of course not. He just laughed when he jumped in our nest. My wife was so upset she swallowed the worms meant for our chicks' breakfast.'

'That's no laughing matter,' said the worm, shuddering.

'Well my dears, I'm sorry if he's caused any trouble, but he'll soon grow out of it,' said the frog. 'Anyway, it shows he's got spirit and I like young frogs to have spirit.'

Besides being spirited the young frog was also very curious about the garden in which he lived. Everything interested him. What was Mrs Prentice doing walking up and down the lawn with a strange machine that seemed to eat the grass? What was Mr Prentice doing with a sharp knife, cutting away at dead branches? What were Katie and Sam doing, sticking little seeds into holes they'd made in the ground, then pouring water over them? And what was Matt doing, hitting small white balls with long metal sticks? (Matt had, for the time being, given up football and taken up golf.) Everything was interesting to the young frog.

'You'll get into trouble if you're not more careful,' said the mole, shaking his head. 'Don't you know that curiosity killed the cat?'

'I'm not a cat,' said the froglet. 'And it's none of your business anyway,' he added rudely.

The frog's mother smiled to see her son, but she did get a little worried when Matt narrowly missed hitting him with a golf club. And when the young frog fell into the lawnmower bag and was buried under a mountain of grass cuttings she took him to one side.

'You must be careful,' she said.

'I *am* careful, Mother. Honestly. Don't fuss.'

And he hopped off, his eyes bulging with curiosity at everything around him.

The Prentices had not yet made any changes to the garden, much to the relief of the animals, insects and birds.

'We'll decide on that later, when we've sorted out the house,' Mrs Prentice said. 'I suggest we just tidy it up for now.'

So Mr Prentice pruned the overgrown rambling roses. Mrs Prentice cut the grass, and the whole family pulled up the weeds in the flowerbeds. Sam had some difficulty in deciding what was a weed and what was a plant.

'When is a weed a weed and not a plant?' he asked.

'When I don't want it in my garden!' Mrs Prentice said.

The squirrel looked up in surprise.

'How can she call it "her" garden?' she sniffed.

All this cutting and pruning and mowing meant that there was a huge pile of garden waste.

'What are we going to do with it all?' asked Sam.

'The pile's taller than Sam and almost as tall as me,' said Katie.

'We'll have a bonfire,' said their father.

The wind was blowing strongly and the fire soon caught. Flames licked around the edges before starting on the branches and twigs. Katie and Sam watched the flames leap high into the air.

They were not the only ones watching. All the animals, insects and birds in the garden took an interest in the bonfire. The mouse worried that his new nest would be burnt. The blackbird coughed and said the smoke wasn't doing his voice any good and bonfires shouldn't be allowed. The squirrel, watching from a high branch on the oak tree, clapped her paws in delight and called the blackbird a spoilsport. The snail curled into her shell and went to sleep, close, but not too close, to the warmth. The frogs retreated to the coolest, dampest part of their pond. And Morgan ran out of the house barking loudly to everyone he met, 'See that fire? My family did that. Burning all the rubbish. My family made that fire you know.'

The young frog was also watching the fire, entranced by the bright red and yellow flames. He jumped closer and closer until he could feel the heat on his body. What, he thought, if I jump right inside? The idea was exciting.

Glancing round, Sam noticed the froglet. He nudged Katie, then squatted on his heels.

'I wouldn't do that,' he said to the young frog. 'Honestly.'

But the young frog, who had been spoilt from the time he was a tadpole, had never listened to advice from anyone. He hopped nearer.

'It's a really bad idea,' Sam said. 'You'll only get hurt.' He cupped his hands to catch the froglet, but he was too late. The froglet had jumped straight into the fire!

And jumped out again, just as quickly, covered from head to foot in hot white ash.

'Mother!' he cried. 'Mother!!!'

He leaped across the grass and dived into the pond.

'Oh my baby, my baby!' croaked the frog, diving in after him.

'Out of the frying pan and into the fire,' said the mole, shaking his head. 'I did warn him.'

'It wasn't a frying pan,' croaked the blackbird sourly.

'But it was a fire,' said the mole smugly. 'Perhaps that's taught him a lesson.'

5

The Mole's Special Friend

The mole was lonely. 'I've no one to talk to.'

'What do you mean, you've no one to talk to?' asked the snail. 'I'll talk to you.'

'You're always moving around.'

'Yes, but very slowly,' said the snail. 'Anyway, you spend all your time tunnelling.'

The mole sighed. 'What I want is someone who's always there to listen to me.'

'I thought you wanted someone to talk to,' said the blackbird, briskly washing himself in the bird bath. 'Not just someone to listen.'

'It's the same thing,' said the mole. 'I talk, they listen. That's what friendship's all about.'

'Friendship's about listening *and* talking,' said the mouse. 'And it's about being loyal and caring – like the ants were when I was caught in the cottage.'

'Oh it was nothing,' said a passing ant modestly. 'Nothing at all.'

'That's what real friendship is,' said the mouse.

The mole smiled in a rather superior way. He thought the mouse was very stupid to have gone inside the cottage in the first place. But then he thought all the animals, insects and birds that lived in the garden were rather stupid. No one was as clever as he was. None of them was fit to be his special friend.

The starling flew overhead.

'The Prentices' car's come back!' she shouted.

'I didn't know it had been away,' said the squirrel.

'Oh yes,' said the starling. 'The family went out earlier. That dog went as well.'

The starling did not like Morgan.

'How very interesting,' said the squirrel in a bored voice. 'I've got better things to do than spend my time worrying about the Prentices.'

'But we should worry,' said the frog earnestly. 'We should indeed. I was only saying to Froggy the other day that the family might drive off in their car and come back with concrete to fill in the pond. I wouldn't put it past them.'

An hour later the family came out of the house. Morgan bounded round them, barking excitedly.

'Mind out, Morgan,' said Mr Prentice, who was carrying a large container. 'You nearly made me drop it.'

The family went to the pond, watched by curious eyes from every tree, bush and blade of grass.

'Here, frog, we've a present for you,' called Katie, catching sight of a frog squatting on a lilypad.

Mr Prentice knelt down and gently tipped the contents of the container into the pond. 'Six healthy goldfish for you to play with,' he said.

'Well!' said the frog, diving into the pond.

The goldfish swam round and round her. They seemed very confused.

'Who are you?' asked one.

'I am a frog,' said the frog.

'Where are we?' asked another.

'You're in *our* pond,' said the frog, puffing herself up in indignation. 'And I think it very rude of the Prentices to buy fish for *our* pond without asking *our* views on the matter.'

One of the fish peered at the frog.

'Hello,' he said. 'Who are you?'

'I've already told you, I'm a frog,' she said crossly.

'You're not a fish – or are you?'

'What's a fish?' asked another.

'If they *had* to buy fish, why did the Prentices buy stupid goldfish?' asked the frog bitterly. 'Whatever will Froggy say?'

'They seem to be getting on okay, don't they?' said Sam, and the family went inside for their tea.

The mole, who had been watching from a

distance, came closer to the pond.

'Oh, goldfish aren't stupid,' he said, anxious to show off his knowledge. 'They just have very small brains. Did you know that goldfish only remember things for two seconds... or is it three...?' he went on in a worried voice. 'I forget.'

'Your brain isn't much better by the sound of it,' snapped the frog.

'Sorry I spoke,' said the mole, in a huffy voice. 'I was only trying to be helpful. I won't in future.'

'Who am I?' asked the third goldfish. 'And who are you?' he said, staring with his large eyes at the mole.

'I am a mole,' said the mole. 'There are twenty-nine different species of mole and we tunnel underground...'

The goldfish lost interest and swam away.

'If only I could find a friend,' the mole said sadly.

The following morning the mole came up for air in the middle of the rose bed. As he screwed up his eyes in the morning light he saw something, straight in front of him...

'Hello,' he said. 'I didn't know there was another mole in this garden.'

The stranger sat upright, a wide smile on its face.

'Have you come to live here, or are you just visiting?' asked the mole, peering at him short-sightedly.

45

The other mole did not speak.

'You're very welcome in my garden,' the mole said. 'All kinds of animals, insects and birds live here but most of them are quite stupid. You look intelligent. Like me.'

The other mole smiled at him.

'I do hope you'll be my special friend,' the mole said.

The other mole continued to smile his big, beaming smile, and said nothing at all.

'Weren't you hoping for a friend who'd listen rather than talk?' asked the blackbird slyly.

'Yes,' said the mole. 'Yes, indeed I was.' He smiled back at the mole. 'I can see that we're going to get along very well. Very well indeed.'

And for a time they did. Whenever the mole

wanted to talk he would visit his friend, who never seemed to leave the rose bed. Whenever the mole wanted advice he would ask his friend, who never offered any, but always beamed approval when the mole made up his own mind.

'Do you know that the mole's found a friend?' the starling tittered to the sparrow.

'And what a friend!' the sparrow tittered back.

'A stone garden ornament!' finished the starling. They both laughed out loud.

The other animals, insects and birds in the garden watched with growing amusement as the mole talked to his friend.

'Should someone tell him?' asked the snail.

'No,' said the blackbird. 'It's too much fun watching.'

'Tell who what?' asked one of the goldfish.

The frog sighed. 'I know some things are sent to try us,' she said, 'but goldfish must be the most trying of all!'

So no one told the mole. He continued to talk happily and never wondered why his friend only smiled and never talked back, until the day when the squirrel cried out, 'There's a snake! There's a snake in the garden!'

'What?' said the worm.

'Where?' said the mole, blinking.

'What garden?' asked the goldfish.

'There!' said the squirrel.

Right in the middle of the lawn, was a long, twisted, green object.

'I d-don't like snakes,' said the squirrel.

'Me neither,' said the worm. 'Tricky things, snakes. You never know where you are with them.'

There was a sudden hiss, and out of the snake's mouth came a spurt of water, drenching the squirrel, the worm and the snail, and knocking the slug clean off his leafy perch.

The mole laughed and laughed and laughed.

'Did you see that?' he said to his friend scornfully, 'did you see that? That's not a snake! That's a hosepipe! Those stupid animals! Trust them to get it wrong.'

'You think you're so clever,' said the squirrel,

furiously shaking off the water, 'but you're not so clever after all. Don't you know that your friend isn't a real mole at all? It's a *stone* one bought as a garden ornament! You can laugh at us now, but we've all been laughing at you for days!'

The mole turned to his friend. Tentatively he touched it with his paws, then with his sensitive nose. It was indeed made of stone.

'And I thought you were my friend,' he said sadly, preparing to burrow down into the soil. 'Perhaps I'm not so clever after all.'

The worm wriggled alongside him. 'I'll be your friend, if you like,' he said. 'I'm not at all clever, but perhaps we tunnelling creatures ought to stick together.'

'Oh thank you,' said the mole gratefully. 'I'd like that.'

'Who's clever?' asked one of the goldfish.

'What's a friend?' asked another.

6

The Biggest and the Best

Winter had come and gone and the flowering trees were now covered with blossom. Green shoots pushed up from the earth. Worms were busy breaking up the soil and hundreds of daffodils waved golden flowers on slender stems. The birds began to return and build their nests.

'Had a good flight?' called the blackbird as two chaffinches flew towards the garden.

'Not bad,' one replied, 'although we were blown off course for a while. It's good to be back.'

They skimmed low over the wall.

'Nice to see the Prentices haven't spoilt the garden,' said one.

'Nice to see the oak tree,' said the other. 'Shall we build our nest in our usual place?'

They flew towards their favourite branch, but

paused in midflight when they saw that a wooden platform had been built along its entire length.

'Whatever is that?' one of them demanded.

'That,' said the squirrel, running along an upper branch, 'is the base for a tree nest for the children. Welcome back.'

The mole coughed. 'I don't actually think they call it a *nest*,' he said apologetically. 'I think they call it a *house* – a tree house.'

'House, nest, it's all the same,' twittered the chaffinch, fluttering around the branch, looking at it from all sides. 'Why build it here? Haven't they enough room in their cottage?'

'I expect they think it will be fun for the children,' said his wife.

'But that's *our* branch!' the chaffinch exploded. 'We've been building our nest there for years.'

'Much better to carry your home about with you, like me,' said the snail from down below.

The worm poked his head up from between two daffodils.

'Hi,' he said. 'Glad you're back. Life's been boring without all you birds trying to catch me. But that's no bad thing,' he added, sliding out of reach of the blackbird.

The chaffinch was not listening. 'It's dreadful!' he spluttered, puffing out his chest. 'It shouldn't be allowed!'

'We could always build our nest on another branch,' his wife suggested.

A blue tit delicately added a final feather to the nest she was busy building under the eaves of the house.

'There's plenty of room here,' she said generously.

'I don't want to build it there,' the chaffinch said sulkily. 'I want to build it *here* – on *this* branch, of *this* tree, in *this* garden!'

'We can't always have what we want,' said the slug smugly, as he chomped his way through some tender young leaves.

The squirrel had been running up and down the wooden platform of the tree house.

'It's not badly made,' she said, 'considering.'

'Considering what?' asked the chaffinch crossly. 'Considering it was made by humans?'

'They're quite good at building,' said the squirrel. 'The cottage has been there for years and years.'

'I'll show them how a nest should be built,' said the chaffinch suddenly. 'I'll build a bigger and better nest than they could ever build! You'll see.'

His wife nodded, too surprised to say anything, for they usually built their nest together. It would make a nice change for her husband to do all the hard work, she thought. She would enjoy the rest.

But the nest the chaffinch built needed hard work from both of them. They spent their days flying backwards and forwards with twigs, leaves, feathers and bits of moss in their beaks until the chaffinch was finally satisfied.

'Well?' he said, pleased with his work. 'What do you think?'

'Impressive,' said the squirrel. 'But why so close to the tree house?'

For the chaffinches had built their nest on the branch directly above it.

'Because I want to show them how to build a good nest,' said the chaffinch.

'You want to teach them a lesson,' said the blackbird.

'Yes,' admitted the chaffinch, 'I suppose I do.'

'And why is it so large?' asked the spider, busily spinning a web in the nearby willow tree. 'Looks a bit unstable to me.'

'He wants to show off,' said the starling. She flew up and peered inside. 'I can't say I'd like anything as big,' she said. 'It's bound to be draughty.' She nodded to the chaffinch's wife. 'You poor dear,' she said pityingly.

The chaffinch's wife did not reply, but sadly thought that the new nest was not as neat or as cosy as the ones they had built in the past.

In the meantime, Mr Prentice, helped by Katie and Sam, had been building the tree house. There had been all sorts of hammering, sawing and nailing.

'Humans are so noisy,' said the chaffinch sourly. 'And dogs,' he added, for Morgan had spent much of his time running round and round the tree, barking excitedly at everyone he met.

'Very clever, my master. He's building a tree house, you know. That means a house...'

'That's up in a tree,' said the squirrel in a bored voice. 'Yes, we know.'

'I'm helping,' said Morgan. He wagged his tail vigorously, and knocked a neat pile of nails straight into the pond.

'It's raining metal!' shrieked the frog. 'Froggy, I said it's raining metal!'

When the tree house was finished, the animals, insects and birds in the garden thought it very fine. Even the chaffinch was impressed, although he would not admit it. Katie and Sam thought it was wonderful.

'It's terrific!' Katie exclaimed.

'Amazing!' said Sam.

'It's fine for the kids,' said Matt in a superior voice, but he was eager to climb up the rope ladder when Katie invited him.

'Carpentry's not my strongest point,' said Mr Prentice modestly. 'But I think it'll last a few years.'

As spring moved into summer, the chaffinch's wife laid four eggs that eventually hatched into chicks. The tree house was used all the time. Katie and Sam spent every day in it after school. Friends came and played and even Matt visited from time to time.

'I do like having those children so close,' the chaffinch's wife said to her husband. 'It's nice listening to their laughter.'

'Next year you'll want a nest right inside their cottage, I suppose,' said the chaffinch. 'I wouldn't get too friendly with humans. They're not to be trusted. They're dangerous.'

That night there was a rustling and the sound of feet padding across the lawn. A row of teeth shone brightly in the moonlight.

'Fox,' whispered the mouse to his family, and they lay shaking in their nest.

Fox, thought the squirrel and scampered to the top of the willow tree.

'Fox,' said the chaffinch to his wife. 'Keep very still and very quiet,' he said to his four chicks, and they all huddled together inside their large nest.

Just then a strong wind began to blow. The leaves on the trees stirred and rustled and the branches creaked. The fox moved to the bottom of the oak tree, looked up... and waited.

'Mum, I feel sick,' said the smallest of the chicks, as a fresh gust of wind made the nest rock alarmingly.

'Hush dear. It will die down in a while.'

The nest rocked again and the chick moved restlessly.

'Mum...'

Then the nest, which was too large to fit comfortably on to the branch, began to tilt.

The fox pricked up his ears and opened his mouth...

... as the smallest chick fell out!

The cries of the chaffinches woke the entire garden. They also woke Sam who glanced out of his window.

'It's all your fault!' the chaffinch's wife cried to her husband. 'If you hadn't built such a big nest our chick wouldn't have fallen out. And now he's probably been eaten!'

Suddenly the garden was flooded with light. Sam had turned on the security lights.

Startled, the fox looked around. He was very puzzled. He had seen the chick fall from the nest. It should have landed right at his feet. Instead, it had disappeared! He blinked. The brilliant light shone straight into his eyes. If he stayed, he might get caught. He slunk away, out of the garden and into the woods. Better luck next time, he thought.

The chaffinches were crying so loudly that they didn't notice Sam quietly climbing the rope ladder to

the tree house. They did not see him pull off his sweatshirt and wrap it gently round the chick, who had fallen on to the platform. The chick shivered slightly, then opened his eyes.

Sam stretched up his hands. And the chaffinches watched in amazement as Sam placed the chick back into his nest, being careful not to touch him with his hands.

'There,' he said. 'You'll be all right now.'

The chaffinch turned to his wife. 'I've been very stupid,' he said. 'I'm sorry.'

His wife made sure her smallest chick was comfortable, then gave him a small peck. 'Yes, you have,' she said. 'There's room for all of us, and if I don't mind sharing our tree with the children I don't see why you should. After all, I'm the one who has to sit here all day keeping the chicks warm.' She gave him another peck. 'You are a silly old thing,' she said gently.

7
The Runaway Rabbit

The quiet of a sleepy summer's day was broken by the sound of voices.

'I wonder what's going on?' asked the starling.

'I expect we'll know soon enough,' said the spider placidly.

'Don't you ever get excited about anything?' demanded the starling.

'Not usually,' said the spider 'Only when a particularly juicy fly gets caught in my web. Otherwise I've seen it all before.'

But even the spider had to admit that she had never seen anything like the strange-looking object that Mrs Prentice was carrying out of the house. It was shaped like an upside down 'V', with a wooden frame and wire mesh walls.

Mrs Prentice was followed by Katie, carrying a

small container of water, and Sam, carrying a small, furry bundle in his hands. Morgan pranced around, barking loudly.

'Be quiet Morgan, you'll frighten him!' said Katie sharply.

Sam bent his head. 'It's only Morgan,' he whispered to the bundle. 'He's our dog. He barks a lot but he's all right really.'

The starling flew overhead.

'It's a rabbit!' she cried.

'It's a baby rabbit,' Morgan barked back. 'He's come to live with us, but I'm not sure where he'll sleep.' He shook his head worriedly. 'He can't share my bed in the kitchen and Peanuts won't like him sleeping on his cushion.'

'You poor thing,' said the bee sarcastically. 'Thousands of us have to live in one hive and we don't have beds or cushions. It's all right for some.'

'Here's a good bit of long grass,' Mrs Prentice said. 'Put him down, Sam.'

Sam put the baby rabbit on the lawn and Mrs Prentice placed the cage over him. The rabbit scuttled into a corner and sat down, trembling.

'He'll soon settle,' she said.

Sam lay on the grass and looked at the rabbit.

'You'll like living here,' he said. 'Honest. Dad's making you a great hutch to sleep in.' He opened a door at the top and gently stroked the rabbit's fur.

'When you've eaten all that nice grass, we'll move you somewhere else.' He looked up at his mother. 'He hasn't got a name, Mum. I can't just call him Rabbit.'

'Peter,' said Katie promptly.

Sam pulled a face. 'Ugh!'

'You named Peanuts, Katie, so I think Sam ought to chose the name for his rabbit,' said their mother.

'Roland, Ronald, Robert...' Sam muttered.

'Boring, boring, boring,' said Katie.

'Katie, you come in with me and leave Sam to think,' said Mrs Prentice firmly, and they went into the cottage.

'Roger?' barked Morgan.

'Rigby?' suggested the starling. 'Like the people who lived here.'

'Not Rigby,' said the mouse, shuddering. 'Makes me think of cats. Why does the name have to begin with "R" anyway?'

Sam rolled over on the grass and stared up at the sky, lost in thought.

'Why does he have to have a name?' asked the spider.

'Why is he in prison?' asked the starling. 'Has he been bad?' She perched on the roof of the cage. 'Why are you in prison, Rabbit?'

The ant scuttled under the edge of the cage.

'It seems a pretty large prison to me,' he said.

'I can't even see the end of it. Or the sides. Are you sure this is a prison?'

Morgan pressed his face against the wire mesh.

'How would you like to be called Rufus?' he asked. 'It's a good name. I was nearly called Rufus, but Mr Prentice thought Morgan was better.'

The rabbit looked at him with frightened eyes.

'You can't call a rabbit Rufus!' said the starling. 'It's not a rabbit-like name at all!'

'Well, you think of something then,' said Morgan.

'I've more important things to do than think of a name for the rabbit,' said the starling.

'Like what?'

'Like rescuing him. He's only a baby. He shouldn't be in prison.'

'Why not?' asked the worm, popping his head up inside the cage. 'It's rather nice in here. Safe. No birds to worry about.'

The rabbit stared at him miserably. 'I want my mummy,' he said.

'Oh,' said the starling. 'Poor little thing. It's cruel keeping you there. Wouldn't you like to fly free?'

'Rabbits can't fly,' said the squirrel scornfully.

Sam sat up and stroked the rabbit with the tip of one finger. 'Aren't you hungry?' he asked. 'Rudolph? No... Russell? Ryan? Look, there's lots of tasty grass for you to eat.'

'Sam! Sam!' It was his mother.

'I've got to go now, Rabbit,' Sam said, getting up from the grass. 'But I'll be back soon. And I'll think of a name for you,' he promised.

'I want my mummy,' said the baby rabbit. But Sam had gone.

An hour later the animals, insects and birds were still watching the baby rabbit.

'It's not fair, keeping him in a cage like that,' said the starling.

'What's not fair?' asked the worm. 'It's very comfortable and he's safe. There's food, water, and a friendly child to look after him. It could be a lot

worse. I wouldn't mind it myself, but no one keeps worms as pets, more's the pity.'

He wriggled into the cage. 'You stay right where you are,' he said firmly. 'Don't even think of escaping.'

'I wasn't,' said the baby rabbit. 'I want my mummy.'

'The family you've come to live with are very kind,' said the mouse. 'Why don't you have a nibble of that nice grass and try and get some sleep?'

'I still think he should be rescued,' said the starling.

'So do I,' said the chaffinch.

'Me too,' said the blue tit.

'But who can rescue him?' asked the spider. 'Me? You? The ant?'

'All we need is a little organization,' said the ant firmly.

'All we need is something larger than us,' said the starling. She thought for a moment, then flew to where Morgan was busily eating his supper.

'Morgan,' she said. 'We need your help.'

Morgan looked up.

'We need you to overturn the rabbit's cage.'

'Why?' asked Morgan. 'It's a nice cage. What's wrong with it?'

'The rabbit shouldn't be in prison and only you can set him free,' said the starling.

Morgan thought for a moment, his head on one side.

'You'll be a real hero, Morgan,' said the starling.

'All right,' Morgan said. He liked the idea of being a hero. 'When I've finished eating.'

'There's no time to waste,' said the starling.

'There's always time for eating,' Morgan said firmly. 'Besides, I'll need all my strength.'

When Morgan had finished his meal, he went over to the cage and stuck the tip of his nose through the mesh. Then he put his paw under the wooden edge and pushed. The cage shifted slightly.

Morgan tried again, this time lifting his paw higher and pushing harder with his nose. The cage wobbled... then tipped right over!

'Hurray!' cried the starling.

'Well done!' said the ant.

'Am I a hero?' asked Morgan, and he ran round and round the garden, barking loudly.

The baby rabbit sat in the middle of the lawn. The garden seemed very large. Shadows were beginning to form under the trees as the sun sank low in the sky. The baby rabbit shivered.

'I don't like it out here,' he said.

'But you're free now,' said the starling, flying up and down excitedly. 'You don't have to stay. You can go anywhere!'

The baby rabbit began to hop slowly towards the flower bed.

'Where's my mummy?'

Morgan's barking brought Sam running out of the house. He stopped when he saw the overturned cage.

'Mum!' he called. 'Mum! My rabbit's gone! He's run away!'

He sat on the lawn and burst into tears.

'I always wanted a rabbit,' he sobbed. 'I loved him.'

Mrs Prentice ran out of the house and put her arms around him.

'Perhaps he went because I couldn't think of a name for him,' Sam cried into her shoulder.

'Oh dear,' said Morgan. 'I think I might have made a mistake.' He put his paw gently on Sam's arm, and nudged him in the direction of the rabbit.

'He can't have gone far,' said Katie and began searching at the other end of the garden.

The baby rabbit stopped. 'Mummy! Mummy!' he called. There was no answer. He turned, looked at Sam, and began hopping back across the lawn.

'I think I'd rather stay here,' the rabbit said.

'Well,' said the starling. 'I wash my wings of the whole affair. I tried to rescue him. But if he's happy to be a prisoner, that's his business. I did my best.'

Sam carried the rabbit into the house, his face wreathed in smiles.

'I've just thought of a name for you,' he said. 'It's Runaway.'

'You can't call him that…!' Katie began.

'I can!' said Sam defiantly. 'Runaway Rabbit. It's a good name and I bet no rabbit's ever been called that before.'

He gave the rabbit a hug, and Runaway snuggled down contentedly in his arms.

8

The Spiders Go to War

'I don't know where you're off to, Matt, but I've a job for you,' said Mrs Prentice firmly as Matt opened the back door. 'It's high time the coal bunker was cleared out. It's in a complete mess.'

'I'm just off to Joe's. He's got a new computer game...' Matt began.

'Games can wait, the coal bunker can't,' said Mrs Prentice even more firmly. 'We need to restock with coal before winter.'

Matt looked at his father, who grinned sympathetically. 'When your mother speaks in that tone of voice, there's absolutely nothing you can do about it,' he said. 'I'll give you a hand.'

So, armed with brooms and shovels, Mr Prentice and Matt descended on the coal bunker and lifted the lid.

One of the large, black, hairy spiders who lived inside blinked at the sudden light. "Ere, what's goin' on? Who's lifted that lid?'

'It's the Prentices,' hissed another spider. 'They're comin' to throw us out!'

'But it's our home!'

'It's their coal bunker.'

'Hey, look at those enormous spiders, Dad!' said Matt. 'If Katie saw them, she'd go mad! She hates spiders.'

'Well, she won't see them,' said Mr Prentice, wielding his broom vigorously. 'Out you go!'

He and Matt swept the spiders and their webs out onto the patio, where they ran round and round in a bewildered fashion.

'What are we goin' to do, chief?' asked one.

'Stop runnin' round and round!' said the largest, blackest and hairiest spider of them all. 'You're makin' me dizzy.'

He led the way to a stack of logs that was piled neatly against the garden wall.

'Now,' he said. 'We're goin' to have to think, and think hard.'

The spiders crowded round him, muttering.

'They've thrown us out of our home!'

'Why did they do it?'

'We never did them any harm!'

The mutterings increased in strength.

'QUIET!' roared their chief. 'I'm tryin' to think!'

The noise subsided.

'Now,' said their chief. 'We've been thrown out of our homes. So we need somewhere to live...' He stopped and thought some more. 'I know what we'll do! We'll invade *their* home an' live there!'

The spiders looked at each other.

'What about those nasty little house spiders?' said one of them. 'They won't like it.'

'They'll say there's no room for us,' said another.

'There's plenty of room!' said the chief. 'We only want somewhere the size of a coal bunker after all!'

'We could always ask them...' suggested one of the spiders.

'And I know what their answer'll be,' retorted the chief. 'No, we've got to take 'em by surprise. A mass attack.' He looked round the group. 'And if those house spiders don't like it, we'll eat 'em!'

'I never liked 'em, anyway,' said a spider. 'Thin little things with hardly a hair on their bodies.'

'Their webs are thin too,' said another. 'Not like our nice, strong ones.'

The spiders began to move towards the house.

'Not so fast!' said their chief. 'We'll wait till the Prentices are indoors. Then we'll take 'em by surprise!'

'We'll creep into their beds. That'll give 'em a surprise!' sniggered a particularly hairy spider. They curled up their legs in pleasure at the thought.

'Now, no talking,' warned their chief. 'We don't want anyone finding out our plans.'

But he was too late. A group of woodlice, nestling deep in one of the logs, had heard everything. They told an earwig, who passed the news on to a snail. The snail told the worm, the starling overheard them, and soon all the animals, insects and birds in the garden knew what the coal bunker spiders were plotting, for the starling never could keep a secret.

Morgan bounded into the house and told Peanuts, and that was how the news reached the spiders who

lived inside Willow Cottage. They gathered together under a floorboard for a council of war.

'We don't want those vulgar, rough spiders coming to live here,' one of the house spiders declared.

'Absolutely not,' said a small spider. 'They're loud and they're common and as for those nasty hairy bodies and big legs, why they'd frighten the Prentices to death.' She shuddered. 'They frighten *me*, and I'm a spider!'

'If they get in, they'll spoil everything,' said a third spider thoughtfully. 'The Prentices have got used to us house spiders. We're quiet, we're clean, we make beautiful webs and we eat flies.'

'So we've got to stop them,' said the first spider. 'Is that agreed?'

'Agreed,' said the spiders, and they laid their plans.

'Whose side are you on, Morgan?' asked the starling, as Morgan went for a run round the garden.

Morgan looked up and ran straight into a spade which Mr Prentice had left stuck in a flower bed. The spade fell with a bang.

'Ouch!' said the worm.

'Side?' asked Morgan. 'What do you mean?'

'Do you support the coal bunker spiders or the house spiders?'

'I don't support either,' Morgan replied. 'Should I?'

'You ought to take sides,' said the starling.

'There's going to be a war between them!'

Puzzled, Morgan ran into the house.

'What's all this about a war?' he asked Peanuts, who was stretched out on the hearthrug.

'It's a lot of fuss over nothing, to be sure,' Peanuts said. 'Live and let live, I say.'

'But the starling says that the coal bunker spiders haven't anywhere *to* live.'

'If you believe that, you'll believe anything,' said Peanuts. 'All that's happened is that their coal bunker was swept out. I like my basket washed from time to time and I daresay you don't object when your kennel is cleaned. There's surely nothing to stop them returning to their coal bunker now it's been swept.'

'But which side ought I to be on?' Morgan asked anxiously. 'I don't know what to think.'

'Thinking's bad for the brain,' said Peanuts kindly, settling himself to sleep. 'If you want my advice, I'd keep well out of it. It'll all blow over.'

Reassured, Morgan went to fetch his lead. It was time for his walk.

That evening, the coal bunker spiders assembled on the patio.

'Right, spiders!' said the chief. 'Go for it!'

They ran on thick hairy legs towards the open patio door. They crawled over the ledge... and then fell back. A stout web had been spun right across the opening.

'Try and get through that!' jeered the house spiders from the other side.

The coal bunker spiders re-grouped and tried again and Morgan, just back from his walk and hearing the commotion, came flying across the lawn.

'Leave this to me,' he barked. 'I'll soon sort it out.'

With a jump, he was through the open patio door, tearing the fine web to shreds. The coal bunker spiders rushed after him into the house.

'Oh Morgan,' sighed Peanuts, from the safety of the garage roof.

The battle did not last long. The house spiders quickly vanished into nooks and crannies, while the coal bunker spiders were soon thrown out by the family.

'We won, didn't we chief?' asked a large black spider, as they returned to the dark of their newly cleaned coal bunker.

''Course we did,' said their chief. 'We taught 'em a lesson. We got into the house, didn't we?'

'You were soon thrown out,' said the starling from a nearby bush. 'And you wouldn't have got in at all if it hadn't been for Morgan.'

'Who'd want to live in a house anyway?' retorted the chief. 'It's much nicer in our bunker. So dark and cosy.'

The house spiders came out of their hiding places. They too felt that they had won.

'It was a good web,' they congratulated one another. 'It held firm against the spiders.'

The animals, insects and birds who lived in the garden were, by and large, pleased that the war was over.

'Life's too short to be fighting,' said the worm.

'Yours will be even shorter if I catch you,' said the blackbird, but the worm only laughed and slipped out of reach.

'I don't know what all the fuss was about anyway,' said the old spider whose strong web, spun between the branches of the apple tree, shimmered in the evening sun. 'There's room for all of us here in the garden.' She watched with hungry interest as a fly flew into her web, then looked round at the animals, insects and birds. 'We've got to learn to live together in peace,' she said.

But not *everything* was at peace inside Willow Cottage.

'I wish you hadn't let all those large, black hairy spiders come into the house!' Mrs Prentice was saying crossly to her husband. 'It took ages to get rid of them.'

'You wanted the coal bunker cleaned,' Mr Prentice said.

'And I gave up my spare time to do it,' Matt added.

'Horrid, black, hairy things,' said Katie, shuddering.

'I'm sure I'll have nightmares about them.'

Peanuts and Morgan lay side by side on the hearthrug.

'I thought I told you not to take sides,' Peanuts murmured to Morgan.

'I didn't,' Morgan said indignantly. 'I was only trying to help.'

Sam sat beside them and kept very quiet indeed. For cupped inside his hands was a very large, very hairy and very black spider.

9

Animals to the Rescue

Peanuts ran out of Willow Cottage, his fur standing on end.

'I can't take any more!' he squealed, as he ran across the patio and jumped onto the roof of the garden shed. 'It's too much for any self-respecting cat, so it is,' he added, collapsing in a heap. 'Oh, my heart! It's not good for me to be runnin' about as if I was half my age and a quarter my size!'

'What's happened?' asked the starling.

But before Peanuts could reply, Sam burst out of the cottage, shouting, 'It's not fair!' He was followed by Mrs Prentice, Katie and Matt.

'Why don't you practise out here?' his mother asked.

'Or in the woods,' said Matt. 'Or anywhere, as long as it's miles away. I've got exams tomorrow and I'm *trying* to revise.'

'Not before time,' murmured his mother.

'Why should *I* have to go out?' Sam demanded.

'Because it's impossible to do anything when you're making that racket,' said Katie.

'It's not a racket!' Sam insisted. 'And I've *got* to practise if I'm to get into the school orchestra.'

'You'll never get into the orchestra in a million years,' said Matt.

'Yes, I will.'

'No, you won't.'

'Yes, I will!'

'Whatever are they arguing about?' asked a passing wasp.

'Now stop that, both of you,' said Mrs Prentice firmly. 'Matt, you get back inside. You've little enough time left for revision as it is. And you can practise here, Sam. It's nice and quiet and you won't bother anyone.'

'He'll bother me,' said Peanuts.

The family went indoors, but Sam soon came back outside, armed with music-stand, music, violin and bow. He was followed by an excited Morgan.

'If he's playing that thing out here, then I'm off to the farm,' said Peanuts. He got to his feet, jumped onto the wall, and disappeared with a disapproving whisk of his ginger tail.

Sam tucked his violin under his chin and swept the bow across the strings. There was a high-pitched, screeching wail.

A song thrush, who had been singing from the top of the oak tree, stopped abruptly and peered down.

'What,' she demanded, 'is that?'

'That's a violin,' said Morgan helpfully. 'Sam's learning to play.'

Another screech.

'I think he's quite good,' Morgan added loyally.

'Then you haven't any taste in music,' said the song thrush sourly. 'I'm sorry,' she went on. 'I *am* sorry, but it's too much. It really is too much. I have a very delicate ear and a very sensitive nature and that noise is just TOO MUCH!'

She flew away, quickly followed by many other birds. They rose like a cloud from every tree and every bush and headed away from Willow Cottage, out of range of Sam's violin. As he continued to play, the snail went into her shell, the squirrel ran into the woods and the worm burrowed far down into the soil. Even the slugs stopped eating and moved to some shrubs at the far end of the garden.

Only Morgan remained, thumping his tail in time to the music. 'That's very good,' he barked encouragingly.

'Shut up, Morgan, will you?' Sam said, frowning with concentration. 'I can't think with you making that noise.'

Morgan bounded off to the pond.

'That's Sam, playing the violin,' he told the goldfish. 'He's very good.'

'Who's Sam?' asked the goldfish.

While the fine weather lasted, Sam played the violin on the patio every day after school.

'He'll drive us all from the garden,' said the squirrel.

'Perhaps it's a plot to get rid of us,' said the blackbird.

'Whatever are we going to do?' asked the snail. 'I can't hide inside my shell all summer.'

'How about getting the woodpecker to drill holes in his violin?' suggested the squirrel.

The starling shook her head. 'Woodpeckers never do anything to help others.'

'I could sting Sam on his hand,' suggested the wasp helpfully, as he buzzed round and round the patio. 'That would put a stop to his playing.'

Everyone thought about this for a moment.

'It seems rather mean,' said the chaffinch at last, remembering how Sam had rescued their baby chick.

'He's a kind boy,' said the mouse, remembering how Sam had wanted to keep him as a pet. 'Even if he's not very good at playing the violin.'

'I don't think we should do anything at all,' said the spider, starting to spin another intricate web. 'He'll soon get tired of it.'

So the animals, insects and birds in the garden of Willow Cottage put up with the screeches, scrapings and wailings as Sam practised on his violin.

His playing soon attracted interest from some children who lived nearby. They took to following Sam home from school, hiding behind the wall, then popping up to laugh and jeer whenever he came out to practise.

'Ow... owhh... owhhh!' cried one as though in pain.

'Give us a proper tune, Sam!' called another.

'Why don't you play something decent, like a guitar?' shouted a third.

Sam ignored them.

They climbed onto the wall, put their hands over their ears, pulled faces and pretended to be sick.

Sam gritted his teeth and played on.

But after a few minutes he couldn't stand it any longer and fled inside.

'Well that's really horrid,' said the wasp.

'Such nasty children! You wouldn't get my froglet

behaving in that disgraceful way,' said the frog.

'Your froglet's behaviour is even worse,' muttered the squirrel, but the frog did not hear her.

'The poor boy's not doing any harm,' said the song thrush, quite forgetting her earlier feelings.

'I think he's beginning to play quite nicely,' said the frog. 'I was only saying to Froggy the other day, "Froggy," I said, "that child is really playing quite nicely now. I can sometimes make out the tune and croak along with it." '

The next day the children were there again, laughing and jeering. As soon as Mrs Prentice came outside they fled, but Sam threatened to give up playing altogether.

'Don't do that,' said Katie. 'I think you're doing really well.'

'Honestly?' Sam asked with suspicion.

'You only set my teeth on edge ten times today. Yesterday it was twelve times,' Katie replied solemnly, then burst out laughing.

Sam took a swing at her with his bow.

'It's the auditions tomorrow, isn't it?' his mother asked. 'You don't want to miss your chance. We'd all be so proud if you got into the orchestra.'

'Any problems and I'll soon see those children off,' Morgan barked. 'I'll take a piece out of their trousers! I'll tear them to pieces!'

'They won't come back,' his mother reassured

Sam. 'If they do, you can practise in the kitchen.'

Matt whistled. 'That's truly heroic, Mum.'

But the next day the children were back again.

'Owwh, owwh, it hurts!' cried one.

The second began to sing, loudly and off-key.

Sam flung down his violin and went over to them. 'Just you clear off, or I'll... I'll...!'

He never got a chance to say any more, for at that moment several things happened at once. The animals came to the rescue!

Morgan came tearing out of the house, growling and barking fiercely. Peanuts jumped onto the wall, hissing and spitting. The wasps buzzed round the children's heads. All the other animals gathered round to watch – the birds twittering, the squirrels chattering, the ants lined up in a row along the patio. The children ran away, without looking back.

'Well?' Mrs Prentice asked when Sam came home from school the next day. 'Did you get into the orchestra?'

Sam nodded and smiled a big, beaming smile. 'Now I'll have to practise even harder,' he said, taking his violin out of its case.

The animals, insects and birds in the garden looked at one another.

'Why ever did we go to his rescue?' asked the squirrel.

10
The Neighbours Come to Call

'Have you heard the news?' shouted the starling, landing on a branch of the oak tree. 'The Prentices are expecting visitors.'

The blackbird winced. 'Must you be so loud?' he asked. 'I've such a headache!'

'If you don't want my news, you've only to say so,' said the starling in a huffy voice.

'It's not you,' said the blackbird. He nodded to where a vigorous tap-tap-tapping could be heard. 'It's the woodpecker. He's been at it for hours.'

The tap-tapping could even be heard inside Willow Cottage. No one was listening though, for Mrs Prentice was making even more noise as she tidied up.

'I don't know why you're bothering, Mum,' said Matt.

'First impressions are so important,' said a flustered Mrs Prentice. 'Katie, for the third time, will you move! How can I clean when you're spread right across the table! And Sam, get your violin out of here. You don't want someone sitting on it by accident, do you?'

'They'd have to be pretty stupid to sit on a violin,' muttered Sam.

'We ought to make an effort – they're our neighbours, after all,' Mrs Prentice went on.

'Why did you invite them?' asked Katie, reluctantly clearing away her things.

'I met Mrs Thomson at the Post Office and she was very friendly. She said she'd wanted to see inside the cottage for a long time, but the Rigbys had been very standoffish. She's got two children, Angela and Damian, and she said how nice it would be if you could all be friends...'

'Oh Mum!' Katie exploded. 'They're probably horrible!'

'You don't *know* that,' said their mother. 'They might be delightful.'

'Yeah, right!'

'Whatever they're like, we've just got to put up with them,' said Mr Prentice, coming into the room. 'Matt, Katie, Sam, I want you on your best behaviour. We've got to impress our new neighbours with our charm, our intelligence, our children... and our animals,' he added, looking at Peanuts and Morgan.

'What's he mean?' asked Morgan anxiously.

'He's being sarcastic,' said Peanuts. 'I think I'll go to the farm. I've already met Damian and I can't say I want to meet him again. He pulled my tail.'

An hour later, the woodpecker was still tapping tirelessly as Mr and Mrs Prentice showed their guests onto the patio.

'Haven't done much to the garden, have you?' said Mr Thomson abruptly. He was a big man with a red face, thinning hair and a very large stomach.

'We like it as it is,' said Mr Prentice.

Mrs Thomson, a thin woman with a long, sharp nose, gazed around enviously. 'We wanted to buy this place,' she said. 'We came a year ago when it was up for sale. But we couldn't afford it.' She sighed. 'We had such plans.'

'We'd have had that down for a start,' said Mr Thomson, nodding towards the willow tree. 'Roots, you know. They spread right under the house. Very dangerous.'

'We like the willow tree,' said Mrs Prentice firmly.

Mr Thomson walked over to heap of fresh soil on the lawn and kicked it with his foot.

'Moles,' he said. 'You'll have to get rid of them, else you'll have no lawn left. I've got some stuff in my shed I could let you have.'

'What sort of stuff do you think that is?' asked the

mole anxiously. He was listening from the safety of a large bush.

Mrs Thomson suddenly cried out, 'Oh, there's a squirrel!' She turned to Mrs Prentice. 'Don't you know they're vermin?'

'What's vermin?' asked the squirrel, busily cracking a hazelnut with both paws.

'Something nasty like me,' said a rat who was slinking along the garden wall.

'I like the squirrel,' said Sam firmly. 'And the mole.'

'You're stupid then,' said Damian, snuffling into a handkerchief. It was the first time he had spoken.

'Squirrels don't belong in the garden,' said Mrs Thomson in a patronizing voice. 'They should be in the woods.'

'I suppose,' said Mrs Prentice thoughtfully, 'that we don't belong in the garden either.'

'Whatever do you mean?'

'Well, this garden is just as much a home to the animals, insects and birds who live in it as it is to us. Why should we try to get rid of them?'

Mr and Mrs Thomson glanced at one another.

'What a very strange idea,' said Mrs Thomson.

There was an awkward silence, broken by Matt and Katie emerging with the tea things.

'Scones!' said Mr Thomson rubbing his hands. 'My favourite!'

'Mine too,' said the ant. 'Come on, chaps!' he called. 'They're having a feast!'

Ants emerged from every crack and crevice.

'Ant powder, that's what you need,' said Mr Thomson, who noticed everything. 'Probably a nest under the patio.'

'We thought it warm enough to sit out,' said Mrs Prentice, 'but we could go in if you'd prefer...?'

'Just as long as there aren't any wasps or flies,' said Mrs Thomson. 'Damian can't stand them, can you, sweetie?'

Damian looked important. 'No, and I don't like dogs, and cats make me sneeze.'

'We've got a cat *and* a dog,' said Sam.

As if on cue, Morgan ran out of the house barking loudly. He bounded up to Damian, his tail wagging and his tongue hanging out.

'Hello,' he said. 'I'm Morgan. Pleased to meet you.'

Damian whimpered and backed into a corner.

'He only wants to be friends,' Sam said.

'Take Morgan indoors, Sam,' said Mr Prentice. 'Not everyone likes his style of welcome.'

'Is there anything you *do* like?' Katie asked.

'I like butterflies,' Damian said after some thought. 'I like pulling their wings off.'

A butterfly, who had been sunning herself on a rose bush, quickly flew away.

After tea the Thomsons were given a tour round the garden.

'You've got slugs,' said Mr Thomson, shaking his head over the lettuces. 'Can't have that. I've got something that'll sort them out. Remind me to drop it round.'

'What's wrong with us eating the lettuces?' demanded the slug. 'We've all got to live, haven't we?'

'I suppose you're too busy to weed properly,' Mrs Thomson said in an understanding voice. 'I do hate weeds, don't you? They make everything look so untidy. We used a very good weed killer in our last house. I'll write the name down for you.'

'Mum says that weeds are only plants you don't want growing in your garden,' said Sam.

'Yes, Sam, thank you,' said Mr Prentice. 'Why don't you and Katie take Damian and Angela to look at the pond?'

On the way to the pond, Angela suddenly stopped.

'I feel sick,' she said.

'You shouldn't have eaten so many scones then,' Katie said bluntly. Angela had eaten twice as many as everyone else.

Damian liked the pond. He picked up a stone and threw it at the frog. It missed.

'Oh! That nasty, nasty boy!' croaked the frog, jumping to the bank.

'Don't do that,' said Sam.

Damian picked up another stone. 'Why not?'

'You might hurt it.'

Damian shrugged. 'So what?' He lobbed the stone and laughed. 'Look! See how it jumps!'

'You wouldn't like stones being thrown at you, would you?' asked Sam.

'It's not the same.'

Damian picked up a third stone, took a step closer to the pond, slipped on the edge, and fell into the water with a loud splash!

'Serves you right,' said Katie.

Damian clambered out, sobbing, and Angela, who had been rather green in the face, was promptly sick.

Later that evening, long after the Thomsons had gone home, the Prentice family sat on the patio and watched the sun setting over the woods at the end of the garden.

'I don't suppose we'll be entertaining them again in a hurry,' Mr Prentice remarked. Morgan barked his agreement.

They sat in silence for a while. The shadows

lengthened and Mrs Prentice brought out a candle. Its flame attracted a moth.

'Oh what a beautiful light!' the moth cried, and she danced around the flame, drawing closer and closer.

Ants scurried busily along the paving slabs, taking away the last crumbs left over from tea. Morgan lay with his eyes closed, his tail twitching from time to time as he dreamed pleasant dreams. Peanuts silently jumped down from the wall and curled up beside him.

Tap-tap-tap...

'It's the woodpecker again!' said Sam excitedly. He turned to his mother and gave her a hug. 'Oh Mum, I do like living here!'

'So do I,' said his mother. She looked round at her family. 'So do we all, I think. Even you Matt?'

Matt shrugged. 'It's cool,' he admitted.

'Better the Prentices than the Thomsons any day,' said the frog with a shudder. 'I was only saying to Froggy that if the Thomsons had bought Willow Cottage we would *certainly* have had to move.'

'I might yet, if that woodpecker doesn't stop tapping,' grumbled the blackbird.

'Why don't you go and ask him?' said the starling.

'I never thought of that,' said the blackbird. He flew out of his nest. 'I suppose we've got to *try* to get on with our neighbours, however hard it is.'

Mrs Prentice sighed. 'It's such a lovely evening, but perhaps we'd better go in. It's getting cold.'

The Prentices took a last look at the garden as dusk fell and slowly made their way into the house.

Sam picked up the candle and blew out the flame. 'Now you won't burn yourself,' he whispered to the moth, as he followed his family inside.

All Lion books are available from your local bookshop, or can be ordered via our website or from Marston Book Services. For a free catalogue, showing the complete list of titles available, please contact:

Customer Services
Marston Book Services
PO Box 269
Abingdon
Oxon
OX14 4YN

Tel: 01235 465500
Fax: 01235 465555

Our website can be found at:
www.lion-publishing.co.uk